Visit us on the Web! randomhouse.com/kids
Educators and librarians, for a
variety of teaching tools, visit us at
RHTeachersLibrarians.com
The Library of Congress has cataloged
the hardcover edition of this work as
follows: Gutman, Anne. [Petite soeur de
Lisa. English.] Lisa's baby sister / Anne
Gutman, Georg Hallensleben. p. cm. —
(Misadventures of Gaspard and Lisa)
Summary: Lisa is very unhappy about
the arrival of her new baby sister.
ISBN 978-0-375-82251-3 (trade)
[1. Babies—Fiction. 2. Sisters—Fiction.
3. Behavior—Fiction.] I. Hallensleben, Georg.
II. Title. III. Series. PZ7.G9844 L1 2003
[Fic]—dc21 2002001999
ISBN 978-0-449-81012-5 (pbk.)
MANUFACTURED IN SPAIN
10 9 8 7 6 5 4 3 2 1
First Dragonfly Books Edition

Lisa's Baby Sister

ANNE GUTMAN · GEORG HALLENSLEBEN

Dragonfly Books —❀— New York

My mom has been pregnant for a very
long time, and I am tired of it. She can't
run to catch the bus. She makes me
carry my own schoolbag.

She's too fat to play on the seesaw with me.
There's a baby in her belly, and I don't like it.

My parents haven't
decided on a name yet.

I told them I have some good names:
Doofus for a girl
or Goofus for a boy.
My dad told me to go to my room.

My best friend, Gaspard, promised me that he would NEVER talk to the baby. And we could pretend that it didn't exist.

But then it happened.
We were leaving school . . .

. . . and there was my grandma with a big smile. "The baby will be born today," she told me. "While we wait, we'll have some ice cream."

Grandma ordered a gigantic ice cream with two little umbrellas for me. "Lisa," she said, "when you were born . . ."

But I'd heard it before, the story of Victoria, my big sister. She was very jealous and she vowed never to talk to me. But now Victoria talks to me all the time, even when cartoons are on.

The ice cream was melting all over the table when Grandma's cell phone rang. She became very excited and she said, "It's a girl! Her name is Lila."

That night, Dad came home without the baby or Mom, but with lots of photos. I didn't want to look at them.

Two days later, Mom finally came home. And the baby, too. Victoria invited some friends over so she could show off Lila. It was as if they had never seen a baby. All the baby did was eat, but they kept saying, "Oh, isn't she cute!"

To annoy them, I played my flute
really loud just outside
the baby's room.

That made Victoria angry with
me, and we started fighting.

But the baby began to cry, so Victoria let go of me. She and her friends stayed in the baby's room all day. They even took more photos. And then I heard Victoria's blond friend say that Lila and I have the same nose and that we look a lot alike.

When everyone left, I went in to look at
the baby. She had a tiny nose that twitched
in her sleep. Actually, she looked like my old
teddy bear, Elliot, only a little cleaner.

She looked content, even when I opened her eyelid to see what color her eyes were.

I picked her up.
She was so little!

And she smelled
very nice.

The next day, I helped my parents push her carriage around the square. Gaspard wanted to help, too, but she's MY little sister!

As we strolled around the square,
I got a great idea.

I'll take Lila to school tomorrow for show and tell. Then everyone will see that I have the cutest little sister in the world! It will be great for Mom, too. It will give her a rest from taking care of Lila.

And that way Mom will
have enough time . . .

. . . to finally finish making my Tyrannosaurus rex costume.